DISCARDED
from
New Hanover County Public Library

The Scoop on
Ice Cream

by Catherine Ipcizade

Consulting Editor: Gail Saunders-Smith, PhD

Consultant: Peggy Armstrong
Vice President, Communication
International Dairy Foods Association

CAPSTONE PRESS
a capstone imprint

Pebble Plus is published by Capstone Press,
151 Good Counsel Drive, P.O. Box 669, Mankato, Minnesota 56002.
www.capstonepub.com

Copyright © 2012 by Capstone Press, a Capstone imprint. All rights reserved.
No part of this publication may be reproduced in whole or in part, or stored in a retrieval system, or transmitted in any form or by any means, electronic, mechanical, photocopying, recording, or otherwise, without written permission of the publisher. For information regarding permission, write to Capstone Press,
151 Good Counsel Drive, P.O. Box 669, Dept. R, Mankato, Minnesota 56002.

 Books published by Capstone Press are manufactured with paper containing at least 10 percent post-consumer waste.

Library of Congress Cataloging-in-Publication Data
Ipcizade, Catherine.
 The scoop on ice cream / by Catherine Ipcizade.
   p. cm.—(Pebble plus. Favorite food facts)
 Includes bibliographical references and index.
 Summary: "Full-color photographs and simple text present fun facts about ice cream"—Provided by publisher.
 ISBN 978-1-4296-6659-6 (library binding)
 1. Ice cream, ices, etc.—Juvenile literature. I. Title. II. Series.
TX795.I63 2012
641.8'62—dc22   2011000372

Editorial Credits
Katy Kudela, editor; Heidi Thompson, designer; Svetlana Zhurkin, media researcher; Sarah Schuette, photo stylist;
   Marcy Morin, scheduler; Laura Manthe, production specialist

Photo Credits
Alamy/Frontline Photography, 4–5; Mantis Mix, 14–15
Capstone Studio/Karon Dubke, cover, 9, 21 (top right)
Corbis/Bettmann, 7
iStockphoto/Tanya_F, 18–19
Library of Congress, 13
Missouri History Museum, St. Louis, 11
Shutterstock/Lori Sparkia, 17; Madlen, 1; Voronin76, 20–21

Note to Parents and Teachers

The Favorite Food Facts series supports national social studies standards related to people, places, and culture. This book describes and illustrates ice cream. The images support early readers in understanding the text. The repetition of words and phrases helps early readers learn new words. This book also introduces early readers to subject-specific vocabulary words, which are defined in the Glossary section. Early readers may need assistance to read some words and to use the Table of Contents, Glossary, Read More, Internet Sites, and Index sections of the book.

Printed in the United States of America in North Mankato, Minnesota.
032011   006110CGF11

Table of Contents

An Icy Cold Snack 4
Inventing Ice Cream 6
How It's Made 12
Imagine That! 16
Make Ice Cream in a Baggie . 21

Glossary 22
Read More 23
Internet Sites 23
Index 24

An Icy Cold Snack

Ice cream can be fruity or nutty.

It can be sweet or sour.

There are so many flavors to try!

Each American eats enough

ice cream to fill 96 cones a year.

Inventing Ice Cream

How did ice cream get its start? Some say Marco Polo brought an ice cream recipe from China to Italy. If true, ice cream is more than 700 years old!

A new ice cream treat began in 1892. One Sunday a New York shop topped ice cream with cherry syrup. Soon people called the treat a sundae.

Ice cream cones became a hit at the 1904 World's Fair. When ice cream cups ran out, a waffle maker rolled waffles to make cones.

How It's Made

Long ago, people used a hand crank to make ice cream. Today electric ice cream makers do most of the work.

Ice cream has cream, milk, and sugar. But ice cream needs air too! As it freezes, ice cream is whipped. Air gets into the mix and keeps the ice cream soft.

Imagine That!

Ready. Set. Go!

Did you know it takes

about 50 licks to

eat an ice cream cone?

In the United States,

vanilla is the best-selling flavor.

But the world is full of choices.

In Japan you can order

green tea ice cream.

Ice cream comes in all flavors. Some people eat garlic, cheese, or bacon ice cream! What kind of ice cream would you make?

Make Ice Cream in a Baggie

In just a few minutes, you can have ice cream. See what fun flavors you can make when you add toppings.

Makes 1 serving

Here's what you need:

Ingredients
1 tablespoon (15 mL) sugar
½ cup (120 mL) milk
¼ teaspoon (1.2 mL) vanilla
ice cubes
6 tablespoons (90 mL) rock salt

Tools
1 sandwich bag
1 gallon zipper bag
scissors
small bowl

Here's what you do:

1. Pour the sugar, milk, and vanilla into the sandwich bag. Seal tightly.
2. Next, fill the large zipper bag half full of ice. Then add the rock salt.
3. Place the sandwich bag inside the large zipper bag and seal the zipper bag tightly.
4. Shake the bag until the mixture becomes soft ice cream. This will take about 5 minutes.
5. Take out the sandwich bag and rinse or wipe it off.
6. Use a scissors to cut a corner off the bottom of the sandwich bag.
7. Squish the soft ice cream into a small bowl. Enjoy as is or add your favorite toppings.

Glossary

flavor—the kind of taste in a food

hand crank—a lever that a user turns in a circle to power a manual ice cream maker

recipe—directions for making and cooking food

sour—having a sharp, acidlike taste, such as a lemon

sundae—ice cream served with one or more toppings, such as syrup, whipped cream, nuts, or fruit

waffle—a type of cake baked in a machine that presses a crisscross pattern into it

World's Fair—a show in which many countries share their arts, crafts, inventions, foods, and other products

Read More

Gibbons, Gail. *Ice Cream: The Full Scoop.* New York: Holiday House, 2006.

Keller, Kristin Thoennes. *From Milk to Ice Cream.* From Farm to Table. Mankato, Minn.: Capstone Press, 2005.

Internet Sites

FactHound offers a safe, fun way to find Internet sites related to this book. All of the sites on FactHound have been researched by our staff.

Here's all you do:

Visit *www.facthound.com*

Type in this code: 9781429666596

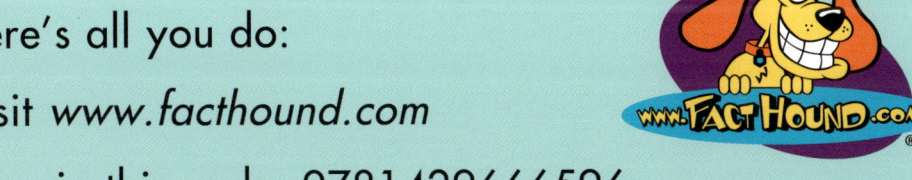

Check out projects, games and lots more at *www.capstonekids.com*

Index

China, 6
cream, 14
flavors, 4, 18, 20
freezing, 14
history, 6, 8, 10, 12
ice cream cones, 4, 10, 16
ingredients, 14
Italy, 6
Japan, 18
milk, 14
mixing, 12, 14
Polo, Marco, 6
recipes, 6, 14, 21
sugar, 14
sundaes, 8
syrups, 8
United States, 4, 8, 18
World's Fair, 10

Word Count: 231
Grade: 1
Early-Intervention Level: 19

CB   12/11